CÚCHULAINN the Hero

A story book to colour

ANNA DONOVAN

ILLUSTRATIONS
JOSIP LIZATOVIĆ

THE O'BRIEN PRESS
DUBLIN

A NOTE ABOUT THE TEXT AND DRAWINGS

TEXT The story of the Táin has been reduced here to its most basic elements in an attempt to introduce children to this famous story in a lively and active way, at a young age. A more developed version of the story can be read in the *Táin*, by Liam Mac Uistin (The O'Brien Press), and details of the way of life of the Celts in *The Celtic Way of Life*, by the Curriculum Development Unit (The O'Brien Press).

DRAWINGS The details in the drawings here have been carefully selected, with the advice of an archaeologist, to reflect the Iron Age Celtic period – it was probably during that period that these epic tales flourished. Objects to be coloured in, such as jewellery and weapons, as well as design features and decorative elements, are in keeping historically with each other. Many of the objects shown may be seen today in the National Museum.

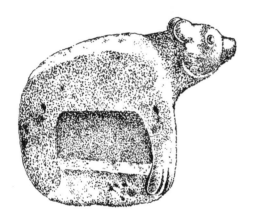 

First published 1996 by The O'Brien Press Ltd.,
20 Victoria Road, Dublin 6, Ireland

The O'Brien Press receives assistance from
The Arts Council / An Chomhairle Ealaíon.

1 2 3 4 5 6 7 8 9 10
96 97 98 99 00 01 02 03 04 05

ISBN 0-86278-454-9

Typesetting, design, layout: The O'Brien Press Ltd.
Printing: Colour Books

design on carved stone

bronze box lid from County Galway

Queen Maeve counted her riches.
Her husband Aillil counted his. They were equal.
But Aillil had a special white bull,
and Maeve did not.

Maeve wanted a bull to match.
'Send to Ulster for the brown bull of Cooley!' she ordered.

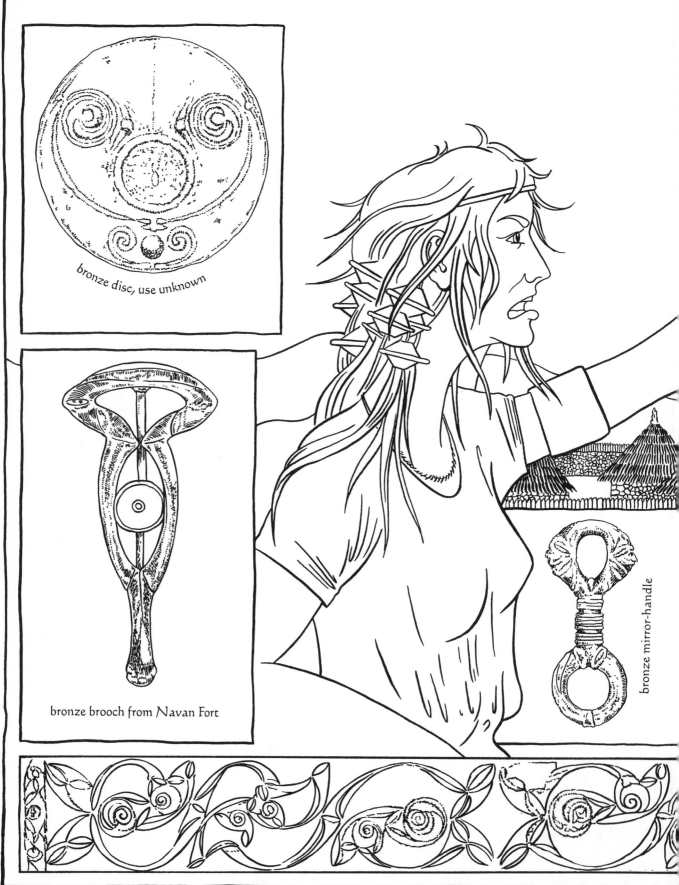

bronze disc, use unknown

bronze brooch from Navan Fort

bronze mirror-handle

gold torc, to be
worn around the neck

clasp

Her servant MacRoth went to get the brown bull.
But Daire, who owned it, would not give it.

designs from gold
Broighter collar

horse-bit from County Monaghan

ornament for use on a horse, found in County Monaghan

'We'll take it so,' said Maeve, angrily.
'We'll go on a cattle raid into Ulster and get the bull.'

6

horse-bit found in County Galway

'Get ready for battle,' Maeve shouted.
A huge army gathered. They set out for Ulster.

Celtic stone idol from County Armagh

cauldron from County Galway

The men of Ulster were under a spell.
They were weak and tired.
They could not fight a battle.

8

But the most famous warrior in all Ulster was CÚCHULAINN.
He was not under the spell. *He* could fight. And he would.

scabbards for holding swords, from County Antrim

Celtic
spearhead

bronze axe-head

Cúchulainn got ready to defend Ulster alone.
He was strong and brave and fearless.

sword-handle, found in the sea

Celtic sword

Maeve sent out warrior after warrior to try to kill Cúchulainn.
But he killed them all, one after the other.
Maeve was furious.

Maeve called on the Goddess Morrigan
to help her against Cúchulainn.
The Morrigan changed herself into a beautiful woman.

She went to Cúchulainn and said:
'Give up the battle for my sake, Cúchulainn.'

Cúchulainn said, 'No.'
The Morrigan told him she would be his enemy forever,
and help kill him some day.
She changed into a huge bird and flew away.

Maeve sent more warriors out against Cúchulainn.
But they were all killed.

When he fought a man named Loch,
Cúchulainn was attacked by an eel.
It wrapped itself around his legs and he almost lost.

But he called for his special weapon,
a magical spear, and managed to kill Loch.
But he could not kill the eel,
for this was The Morrigan in magic shape.
It fled – for now!

Cúchulainn was tired and wounded,
and angry that so many fought against him.
He shook his spears, swung his sword,
and shouted the warrior's shout.

Then he slept for three days to recover from his wounds.
While he slept, the boy warriors from Ulster
fought Maeve's warriors – and lost.

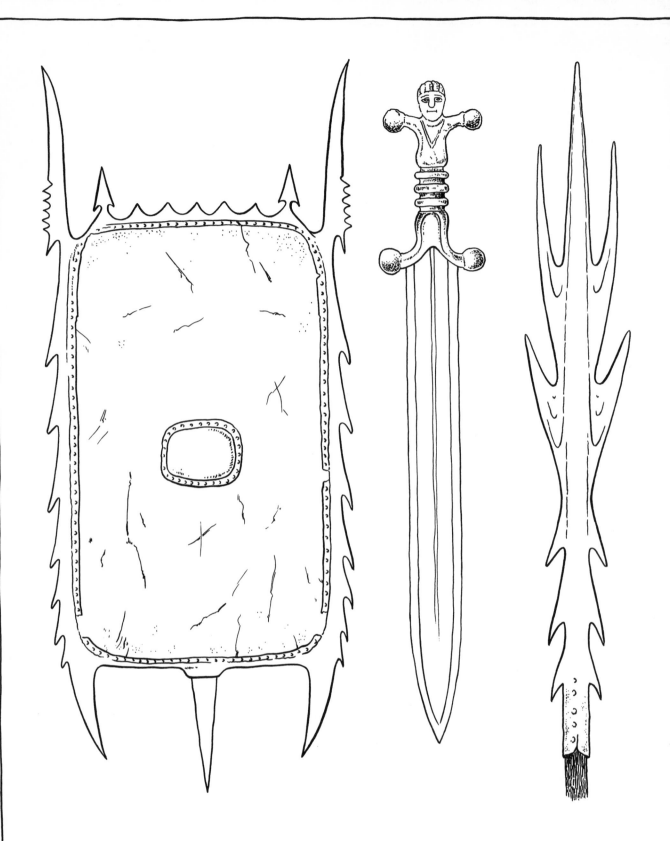

Cúchulainn woke ready for battle again. He was angry at what had happened to the boys. He dressed for the fight with his flashing sword, his many-pronged spear, and his dark red shield with the razor-sharp edges.

He got ready his chariot too.
The sides and wheels had cutting blades,
and the front and back had tearing edges.

He charged into the enemy camp, causing havoc. Tents were torn apart. Warriors died right, left and centre.
Maeve hid in terror. Half her army was gone when Cúchulainn had finished.
But Maeve did not go home.

Maeve sent for the best warrior of all, Ferdia.
Now, Ferdia was Cúchulainn's friend
and did not want to fight him.
But in the end he was forced to do it.

On the first day, Cúchulainn and Ferdia fought
with shields and spears.
After the fight they tried to heal each other's wounds
and they ate a meal together.

The second day was the same.
On the third day the fighting was so fierce
that they could hardly move afterwards.
That night they stayed apart.

On the fourth day they fought in the river.
Ferdia was beginning to win!
Cúchulainn called for his special magical spear.
He shot it at Ferdia.

The spear went through Ferdia's body, and he lay in the river, dying.
Cúchulainn lifted his friend to the bank,
and fell down, exhausted, beside him.
Ferdia died in Cúchulainn's arms, and Cúchulainn wept.

The men of Ulster woke from their spell, and went into battle.
Though he was tired and worn out, Cúchulainn went with them.

First Maeve's men were winning, then the Ulstermen.
In the end, the Ulstermen were driven back to Ulster
and Maeve got her brown bull.
But that was not the end!

When the brown bull met Aillil's white bull, they too fought.
The brown bull won, killing the white bull, then he ran away.
So, in the end, nobody had any special bull!

Other Books from The O'Brien Press

Look out for another story book to colour:

GULLIVER

Frank Murphy

Illustrated by Josip Lizatovic

Swift's famous story in simplest form to enjoy and to colour. Meet Gulliver and travel to the land of Lilliput where Gulliver is a giant among tiny people.
£3.50 PAPERBACK

ART, YOU'RE MAGIC

Sam McBratney

Illus. Tony Blundell

Art thinks everyone will love him if he wears a butterfly tie. But all it does is get him into trouble!
£3.99 PAPERBACK

THE LOUGH NEAGH MONSTER

Sam McBratney

Illus. Donald Teskey

You've heard of Nessie? This is her cousin, quietly passing the centuries hidden under Lough Neagh. Until Nessie comes to visit!
£3.99 PAPERBACK

THE KING'S SECRET
The Story of Lowry Lynch

Patricia Forde

Illus. Donald Teskey

Lowry Lynch has a BIG SECRET – and anyone who cuts his hair must die! What can Seamus the barber do about it?
£3.99 PAPERBACK

THE LEPRECHAUN WHO WISHED HE WASN'T

Siobhán Parkinson

Illus. Donald Teskey

A tall tale about Laurence, tired of being small and uncool, who meets Phoebe, who is tired of being large and uncool!
£3.99 PAPERBACK

TOMMY, THE THEATRE CAT

Maureen Potter

Illus. David Rooney

This is a story about the cat who lives in the theatre and gets involved in the show. Based on a real cat whom Maureen worked with!
£3.95 PAPERBACK

THE FIVE HUNDRED

Eilis Dillon

Illus. Gareth Floyd

Luca buys his heart's desire, a Fiat five hundred. But when it is stolen his life becomes dangerously exciting!
£3.95 PAPERBACK

THE WOODLAND FRIENDS SERIES

THE OWL WHO COULDN'T GIVE A HOOT!

Text and Illus. Don Conroy
Owls hoot, don't they? So what's happened to Barny Owl's hoot? The woodland friends try to solve the problem!

THE TIGER WHO WAS A ROARING SUCCESS

Text and illus. Don Conroy
A tiger in the woodlands? Whatever's happening?

THE BAT WHO WAS ALL IN A FLAP!

Text and illus. Don Conroy
Another strange creature turns up in the woodlands to puzzle all the friends.

THE HEDGEHOG'S PRICKLY PROBLEM

Text and illus. Don Conroy
Harry Hedgehog is bored, but when he joins the circus he ends up in a prickly situation! Can the friends rescue him?
ALL £3.99 PAPERBACK

ORDER FORM

Please send me the books as marked
I enclose cheque / postal order for £......... (+ £1.00 P&P per title)
OR please charge my credit card
☐ Access / Mastercard   ☐ Visa
Card number ☐☐☐☐ ☐☐☐☐ ☐☐☐☐ ☐☐☐☐
EXPIRY DATE ☐☐☐☐

Name: ....Tel: ....
Address: ....
....
Please send orders to : THE O'BRIEN PRESS, 20 Victoria Road, Dublin 6.
Tel: +353 1 4923333 Fax: + 353 1 4922777